THE MAGIC KINGDOM

Margaret D. Clark

Published by New Generation Publishing in 2013

Copyright © Margaret D. Clark 2013

First Edition

The author asserts the moral right under the Copyright, Designs and Patents Act 1988 to be identified as the author of this work.

All Rights reserved. No part of this publication may be reproduced, stored in a retrieval system or transmitted, in any form or by any means without the prior consent of the author, nor be otherwise circulated in any form of binding or cover other than that which it is published and without a similar condition being imposed on the subsequent purchaser.

www.newgeneration-publishing.com

 **New Generation Publishing**

AUTHOR'S NOTE

I live in a big Victorian house by the sea with my family and Tess our Labrador. We all live happily together.

I have seen nature, sprites, they look like little fairies, in the forests near my home, and I have also seen little goblin-like creatures busily working away in the countryside.

It is a marvellous experience to be able to see these magical beings that do exist in the nature kingdom.

Margaret D Clark

CONTENTS

1	MIRANDA RUNS AWAY	1
2	THE MAGIC KINGDOM	8
3	THE INTRUDER	19
4	THE LONG JOURNEY	27
5	THE ICY KINGDOM	36
6	PEGASUS FLIES AGAIN	43
7	THEY RUN FOR THEIR LIVES	53
8	THE KINGDOM OF WITCHES	60
9	THE LONELY GIANT	69
10	THE WITCHES' CASTLE	73
11	THE RESCUE	77
12	PARTY TIME	83
13	SAFE HOME AGAIN	86

CHAPTER ONE
MIRANDA RUNS AWAY

'Even the birds have arguments sometimes,' said a voice.

Startled, Miranda looked up into the leafy branches of a big old oak tree and saw a little elf sitting on a branch watching her. He had twinkling brown eyes and was dressed all in green like the forest. He wore a little pointed hat and cherry red boots that curled up at the toes.

She stared at him in amazement.

'What ails you, little missy?' he said, jumping down to join her.

'Oh, please go away and leave me alone.' The tears ran freely down her face and her bottom lip wobbled.

'I was only trying to be helpful,' he said. 'But if that's how you feel, I'll be on my way.'

'I've run away from home,' she sobbed. Her face was all blotched from crying.

'You need help,' he said.

He invited her to tea.

'I still have some delicious chocolate cake left we can share, and my homemade berry juice goes down a treat,' he added kindly. 'My name is Pip,' and he smiled widely at her.

'I'm called Miranda.'

'That's a pretty name. I once knew a little fairy princess. She was called Miranda too.'

'You expect me to believe that?' she said, beginning to cheer up. 'I might as well come with you. After all, I have nowhere else to go.'

With an air of mystery about him, Pip began playing his flute. The music echoed eerily around the hillside. It made Miranda feel very tired. Her eyelids began to close and she had the feeling she was floating through the air. The music came to an end. Pip had stopped playing and Miranda woke up.

She was in a strange land.

'Oh, Pip, what have you done?' she cried in alarm. 'Where am I?'

'We are in The Magic Kingdom. But this isn't right.' He looked dumbfounded.

A grey mist covered the countryside and it was bitterly cold. Hills, mountains and trees had all turned a ghostly white.

'It's not at all how it should be.' Pip was stunned. His face was as grey as an elephant's back.

'There's danger everywhere, I can feel it in my bones.' He suddenly saw the witches flying towards them on broomsticks.

'What are they doing here?' he cried in horror.

Miranda saw them too. 'The witches are coming! The witches are coming!' she cried, with a look of panic.

'Quick, Miranda, we must hide!'

They dived for cover, hardly daring to breathe until the witches had gone, when they came climbing out of their little hidey hole beneath a gooseberry bush.

'Nasty loathsome creatures,' Pip muttered.

Miranda was shivering with shock. 'I don't like it here,' she said, in a frightened little voice. 'I want to go home.'

Pip stared at her in dawning horror. 'Oh dear, oh dear,' he cried. 'What have I done? I can't send you home now, Miranda. The witches would come and find us. Let me explain,' he said quickly, seeing her white and shaking standing beside him. 'If I played my flute now, the witches would be able to come and find us, just like that.' He flicked his fingers in the air.'

She stared at him wide-eyed with horror.

'Please do forgive me for bringing you here, Miranda,' he said, sorrowfully. 'There is nothing I can do now.' He looked deeply troubled.

She was very upset.

'C'mon, Miranda, we can't stay here. Let's go find my friends.'

They headed off into the forest. The icy ground crunched beneath their feet as they hurried along.

'It used to be such a pretty place,' explained Pip, with great sadness. 'I only popped out to visit the world of humankind, and when I come back everything's changed, and it's like this, all cold and horrible.' He sighed deeply. 'The sun should be shining and the trees in blossom with pretty flowers growing everywhere, and now look at it,' he grumbled. 'I have no doubt in my mind that the witches are to blame.'

They came upon a little grey mouse lying on the ground.

Pip gently picked it up. 'And what have we here?' he said, tenderly. 'The poor creature is freezing to death,' he said, sadly, holding the tiny mouse gently in the cup of his hands. He began to blow his warm breath onto the lifeless little body.

The little mouse suddenly twitched and came to life.

'What do you think you're doing? I was on my way to Heaven, where all my ancestors are, and now you've spoilt it by bringing me back to life.'

'Well, if that's all the thanks I get. I'll leave you here,' Pip said bluntly.

'Oh, I might as well stay here now, seeing as you've gone to the trouble of saving me. I don't want to appear ungrateful, so if you don't mind telling me your names we can get on friendly terms.'

Miranda stared in astonishment. She had never heard a talking mouse before.

'I'm Pip.'

'And I'm Miranda.' She couldn't keep the excitement out of her voice.

'I'm called Tiny Mouse, after my great, grandmother. Please forgive my rudeness earlier. You both seem very nice, if I may say so.'

They both smiled at her.

'We must journey on,' said Pip. 'We have urgent business ahead.'

'Oh, please take me with you. I promise I will be no trouble.'

Tiny Mouse was very afraid.

'The matter's settled, then.' Pip looked down on the little mouse with such compassion. 'Do you happen to know why the weather is so cold?' he asked, worriedly.

'The witches have done this,' cried Tiny, angrily. 'I don't know what they're up to, but we are all going to be dead as driftwood if this keeps up. It's so cold nothing can survive and there's nothing to eat. There's no one about to play with any more and all my friends have gone to I don't know where.' The little mouse shook with fear.

'The witches have no business here,' cried Pip. 'This used to be such a happy place until they came.'

'Calm down, Pip,' said Miranda suddenly. 'You are shouting loud enough for the whole world to hear.'

'Oh dear, oh dear,' he groaned. 'I'm forgetting my manners. All this has given me quite a turn. Do please forgive me.' He looked down at the little grey mouse. 'I can pop you into my pocket if you would like me to. I'm sure you will like it in there,' said Pip kindly, his earlier outburst forgotten. 'And you can pop your head out to have a look around whenever you feel like it.'

'Yes, please,' cried Tiny Mouse excitedly. 'I would like that very much.'

'It can be your new home,' he said, smiling.

Tiny Mouse was quickly popped into Pip's top pocket, watched by a grinning Miranda.

They set off once more along a winding footpath that led them deep inside the forest. No birds sang in the white coated trees and no little creatures could be heard scurrying about in the undergrowth. There was not a cheep of a little bird to be heard. The forest was still and as silent as a graveyard.

They were hurrying along.

'Please slow down, Pip,' panted Miranda, breathlessly. 'You are going so fast I can hardly keep up with you.'

'Oh, dear, I'm sorry, Miranda. 'I'm jiggly puffed too,' he admitted.

'That's a new word,' she said, suddenly smiling.

'Not to me it's not.'

They slowed down and began to walk at a more leisurely pace.

'Would you mind telling me why you ran away from home, Miranda?'

'I couldn't think what else to do,' she said, miserably. 'I was so desperate to get away.'

'Why don't you start at the beginning,' he suggested kindly. 'It's a very good place to start.' He smiled encouragingly.

'I live at home with my parents and my little brother Anthony. He's cute, you'd like him, Pip.' She smiled softly to herself. 'Do you know what he likes to do?'

'No, I don't.'

'He likes me to push him on our swing in the garden.'

'I think I'd like that very much too,' said Pip, smiling.

'We had to move house when Daddy got a new job. He called it a career move. We live in the country now. It's a long way from where we used to live. It's too far away for my friends to come and see me and I have no one to play with. The school I go to now is horrible, everyone is so nasty to me,' she cried bitterly.

Pip looked upset. 'What happened to you, Miranda?' he asked gently, his face full of concern.

'The children at school are spiteful to me and call me nasty names. My hair is pulled until my head hurts and it makes me cry. They won't let me play with them and I have no one to talk to. Oh, I hate it and I'm never going back!

'Oh, Pip, I'm so unhappy.' The tears began to flow.

'Oh, please don't cry, Miranda. I can't bear to see you so unhappy.' He passed her his red spotted handkerchief. 'Bullying is a very nasty business,' cried Pip, angrily. 'Dry your tears, Miranda, nobody will bully you here.'

'Thank you, Pip.' She dabbed at her eyes.

'I'm sorry for your troubles. As I see it,' he said thoughtfully, 'there comes a time in all our lives when we have to stand up to the bullies. I will be your friend, if you would like me to be.'

'I'd like that very much. I'm glad we met, Pip. I've never had a friend like you before.'

It made Pip smile. 'No, suppose not.'

CHAPTER TWO
THE MAGIC KINGDOM

'It's not far now,' he said, eagerly putting a spurt on. 'C'mon, Miranda, we're nearly there.'

They reached a clearing in the forest and stopped to stand and stare. The little village was burnt to the ground, and only one thatched cottage remained standing. The fire hadn't touched it, because it stood well back from the others.

'Who has done this dreadful thing?' cried Pip angrily. 'And where are all my friends?' He looked wildly about him.

The place was deserted. There was not a soul to be seen anywhere.

'Look, Pip,' whispered Miranda, pointing to the little cottage. 'Somebody must still be in there.'

A thin column of smoke drifted slowly up from the little cottage chimney.

'That's old Ma Thackeray's cottage,' Pip whispered. 'Come on, let's take a look.'

They sneaked up to the cottage wall.

They could hear voices coming from the slightly open window and quickly peeped in. A group of witches were crowded around a big black cauldron that dangled over a brightly burning fire. The contents spluttered and bubbled over onto the leaping flames, making the blaze spit and hiss.

The witches were busily making a secret potion as they weaved their magic spell and chanted evilly around a big black cauldron. 'Hocus- Pocus-Diddle-Dum-Dee…'

A little fairy was tied to a chair at the back of the room sobbing pitifully. A witch suddenly looked in their direction. She began to sniff the air suspiciously.

They didn't stop running until they reached the shelter of the trees.

'Oh, Pip, I can't believe what I've just seen.' She was shaking like a leaf and as white as a daisy.

'Oh, whatever next?' he cried.

'Oh, the poor little fairy,' sobbed Miranda. 'How could they be so cruel?'

'I must get my thinking cap on and try and think of a way to save her, Miranda.'

'I'll save her,' cried Tiny Mouse, bravely peeping out of Pip's top pocket. 'I'm so small they won't even know I'm there. I can chew her ropes and set her free faster than you can blink an eye.' She tried to look very fierce.

Miranda stared at the brave little mouse in awe. A huge explosion suddenly shook the trees all around them and made the ground shake.

They all jumped with fright.

'Oh, what was that, Pip!' screamed Miranda, looking madly around as though expecting at any moment a witch to pounce on them.

'Wish I knew,' he said, trembling beside her.

The brave little mouse dived back into Pip's pocket with a tiny squeak of fear. As time passed and nothing else happened they began to feel less terrified.

'I suppose that was those silly witches,' muttered Pip. 'They think they can come here and do just what they like. Well, we'll see about that.' He looked ferocious as he said it, as though he had some plan up his sleeve.

'What can you do to stop them?'

'I'll tell you what I'll do,' he said, with great determination. 'I'm going to stop them from injuring that sweet little fairy. In fact, I'm going to rescue her from their evil clutches.'

She stared at him.

'I must save that little fairy if it's the last thing I ever do.'

'I'll help you, Pip, but,' she added thoughtfully, 'I'm not very brave. I'm even afraid of my own shadow sometimes.'

'C'mon then,' he said, with a grim look.

They went silently back through the forest.

'I hope those rotten old witches have blown themselves up,' muttered Pip wickedly.

Miranda suddenly felt as if she was in some terrible nightmare and would wake up at any moment, and find herself back home in her nice warm bed. They reached the clearing in the forest, and gasped at what they saw.

'Those bungling idiots have set the cottage on fire,' muttered Pip.

'Oh, dear,' cried Miranda, horrified. 'We'll never save her now!'

Another loud explosion almost deafened them. Pip and Miranda clapped their hands over their ears to shut out the dreadful noise.

The witches suddenly tumbled out of the little cottage. They made the most awful racket, caterwauling and shrieking loudly, as they pushed and shoved one another out of the way while the fire licked greedily at their black gowns and pointed hats. Then, one by one, they jumped on their broomsticks and flew quickly high up into the air and over the tree tops and out of sight.

'That's the last we shall see of them,' said Pip, smugly. 'And I hope they have burnt their bottoms off,' he added rudely.

They could hear faint cries for help coming from inside the burning cottage. The little fairy was still trapped inside. She had been left there to die.

'HELP! HELP! Oh, please, someone help me!'

The cries were getting weaker. Time was running out.

'Take Tiny for me, Miranda.'

Pip dashed off.

The fire had a good hold, flames leapt high into the air, like some fiery dragon, and dense black smoke was everywhere. Pip ran courageously into the blazing inferno. Miranda stood a safe distance away as she held the little mouse close to her heart. They were both petrified as they stood there waiting for him to come out. Then suddenly a blackened figure came running towards them. The little fairy was slung over his shoulder. She was all limp and lifeless.

'Oh, Pip!' sobbed Miranda, tears streaming down her face. 'I thought you were going to get burnt alive and I'd never see you again.'

'Run, Miranda, run!' he cried. 'Get away from here! Get away from here!'

They ran for their lives as the cottage exploded like one enormous firework, sending sparks shooting out all over the place.

They didn't stop running until they were safely away. Pip put the little fairy down as she quickly came to her senses. They all gave a sigh of relief. She wasn't dead.

Two emerald green eyes looked up at Pip, adoringly. 'My hero,' she said, in a sweet little voice. 'Who are you?'

'I'm Pip,' he said, brimming over with happiness that she was alive.

'You saved my life.' Her wings fluttered gently.

'I thought I was going to die when he didn't come out,' confessed Miranda. 'My heart was beating so fast I thought it was going to burst,' she admitted. 'I have never known anyone so brave in all my life.'

'It was the bravest thing I have ever seen,' agreed Tiny.

They all looked at Pip admiringly.

'Oh, it was nothing. Anyone would have done the same,' he said, blushing furiously, and suddenly feeling very embarrassed by all the attention he was receiving.

He brushed at his clothes, which were smoke blackened from the fire. His face and hands were dirty too.

'Oh dear,' he said. 'I could do with a swim in the stream.'

Miranda looked amused.

The sweet little fairy gave a tinkling laugh. 'I'll see to that,' she said. Her wings fluttered gently as she chanted a little verse. 'Whoosh, Whoosh. Go away, dirty.'

Pip felt himself covered in soap suds as the dirt and grime began to melt away. He was squeaky clean, and so was the little fairy, without even getting wet.

'Wow,' said Pip, smiling. 'That was fantastic. Thank you.'

'It was nothing,' she cried.

Miranda was amazed by all she saw.

The little fairy gave Miranda a curious look. 'What is your name?'

'Miranda,' she said shyly.

'You don't belong here,' she said. 'You are a human child, are you not?'

'I think so.'

'How did you get here, if you don't mind my asking?'

'I don't mind,' she said. 'Pip brought me here.' She explained the reason why.

'He has a heart of gold, hasn't he?'

'I'm glad he's my friend,' she said.

'And who, may I ask, are you?' asked the little fairy, gazing sweetly at the little mouse sitting in the palm of Miranda's hands, looking boldly out.

'I'm Tiny; Tiny by name and Tiny by nature. Pip saved my life too.'

Pip smiled and gently took the little mouse from Miranda. He stroked her lovingly before returning her to his pocket. 'In you get,' he said, with a wide grin. 'At least you will be safe in there and I know where you are.'

'All this excitement has made me very tired,' said Tiny, her whiskers twitching as Pip gently lowered her into his top pocket.

'Would you mind telling us your name and where you are from?' Pip asked the little fairy.

'I'm Pansy Poppet, and I live in Bumble Bee forest. I was gathering dew drops for a fairy spell when I was captured by those horrible witches. They threatened to chop off my wings so I couldn't fly.'

'The filthy beasts,' muttered Pip.

'Oh, how horrible,' cried Miranda.

The trees were on fire all around and the smell of burning wood was very strong and sparks were shooting out all over the place. Thick black smoke soon had them coughing.

Pip realised the danger they were in. 'C'mon, run, before we are trapped by the fire.'

They ran for their lives. They didn't stop until they reached the fast flowing river and hurried over the brick built bridge to safety.

'We'll be safe here,' said Pip.

They stopped to rest and catch their breath. They could see a log cabin peeping through the trees a little way ahead. It was the woodcutter's hut and a welcome sight. They quickly hurried towards it and found the door unlocked and stepped inside.

'It's empty,' said Pip, gazing about him. 'I wonder where Theodore has gone. I hope nothing has happened to him. He's the best friend anyone could have and always welcomes visitors, so he won't mind if we make ourselves at home.'

They all looked around and saw a sofa and three comfortable armchairs spread about the room. A highly polished wooden table stood beneath the window with four wooden chairs around it.

The brick-built fireplace was cold and empty; the fire had long since gone out. Nearby stood a basket full of logs and newspaper cuttings.

Pip went over to it. 'I'll soon have a fire going,' he said, making himself busy.

Miranda sat down in one of the armchairs. She suddenly longed for home. She missed her warm loving family, and their pet poodle. She wondered if Patch was missing his little mistress as much as she was missing him. The fire was soon burning brightly in the hearth. It gave off a rosy glow around the room and cheered everyone up enormously.

'All we need now is something nice and tasty to eat,' said Pip, rubbing his hands together.

'That would be nice, Pip. I'm really hungry,' confessed Miranda.

'I'll go and raid the larder. I'm sure we can have a slap up meal made in no time.' He turned to leave the room.

'I'll come with you,' said Miranda, getting up.

'Me too,' said Pansy Poppet, eagerly following them.

'Theodore always keeps a well stocked larder,' said Pip, with a grin.

They stood staring around the neat little kitchen.

Pip was the first to open a cupboard door and found it was as empty as a crow's nest when it had been burgled. They searched in all the other kitchen cupboards but they were empty too, apart from a small piece of dried up cheese which Pip gave to Tiny, who gratefully nibbled away at it.

Miranda saw a biscuit tin lying on its side beneath one of the many chairs that were scattered about. She removed it from its hiding place expecting it to be empty, but when she opened it she was astonished to find it was full of delicious looking chocolate biscuits.

'You'll never guess what I've found,' cried Miranda, smiling. She held the tin out for them all to look in.

They all peered greedily in.

'Wow! This is fantastic, Miranda,' cried Pip, delightedly. 'At least we won't go hungry,' he said with a big grin on his face.

'Yummy, yummy,' cried Pansy Poppet in delight and her little gossamer wings fluttering excitedly.

'Anyone would think we'd found buried treasure,' cried Miranda, laughing.

They were all eager to tuck in.

'I think we should go and sit down at the table and eat properly,' said Miranda, bossily. 'Do you think you can find a tablecloth anywhere, Pip?'

They quickly hunted one out and the table was set. A water jug was quickly found and filled to the brim with fresh clear water from the tap and glasses were filled. They all took their place at the table as they settled down to enjoy their supper.

The chocolate biscuits were soon eaten.

'That was the best meal I've ever tasted,' said Pip, rudely licking the last bit of chocolate from his fingers.

'Delicious,' agreed Miranda, suddenly yawning and quickly hiding it behind her hand.

'Sleepy time,' said Pansy Poppet, smiling sweetly at Miranda. They were good friends.

'It's way past my bedtime too,' agreed Pip. 'Come on,' he said, jumping down from his chair, 'I'll lead the way.'

They followed him out of the room and up the little wooden staircase until they reached the top. There were two doors opposite each other.

Pip opened one door and looked inside. He exclaimed loudly, 'If that's not a sight for sore eyes, I'll swallow a tortoise.'

Miranda was overjoyed when she saw the two ready-made-up little beds complete with nice warm blankets on to keep out the cold. All she had to do was climb into bed. Pip opened the door opposite and saw a smaller bedroom with one neatly made-up little bed in.

'You and Pansy take that bedroom and I'll sleep in here with Tiny. Let's all try and get a good night's sleep,' he suggested, adding, 'I'm so tired I could sleep on a moonbeam.'

Miranda chuckled. 'See you in the morning, then. Goodnight Pip, goodnight Tiny.'

'Nighty night,' sang Pansy Poppet back.'

'G'dnight, Miranda, and you too, Pansy Poppet,' he said with a smile before closing the door softly behind him.

They were all soon tucked up in their little beds and sleeping soundly. Somewhere an owl hooted.

CHAPTER THREE
THE INTRUDER

Startled out of a deep sleep, Pip was suddenly wide awake and alert to danger. He could hear someone moving about downstairs. He was suddenly filled with a great terror. He quietly tidied the clothes he had slept in and tiptoed from the room as silent as a ghost.

He had to warn the others before they were discovered. He was just about to alert them to danger when their door suddenly flew open and Miranda stood there with Pansy Poppet beside her.

Two white little faces looked out.

'Shush,' Pip put a finger to his lips and whispered a warning. 'We have an intruder in our midst.'

'I know,' she whispered. 'We heard it too.' She beckoned him in.

Pip stepped silently into the room. They were trembling with fear.

'What are we going to do, Pip?'

They whispered together.

'As I see it, there's only one thing we can do. We must go down and tackle the intruder.'

They gazed at him in terror.

'It's the only way. We must act quickly, before we are discovered.'

There was a thoughtful silence. They knew he was right. There were nods of agreement.

'Right then, let's go for it,' said Pip, looking grim. He opened the door and peeped out. 'All clear,' he whispered.

They all left the safety of the room and made their way downstairs. Tiny was safely tucked away in Pip's top pocket. They made their way silently down the wooden staircase. They soon reached the bottom. Pip put a finger to his lips as a warning not to make a sound. They could see someone moving stealthily about in the shadows. They began to creep up behind him when suddenly he turned around and saw them.

'Quick! Grab him!' cried Pip. 'Don't let him get away!'

They rushed at him with murderous looks on their faces. Before they could reach him he flopped to the floor like a rag doll. They gathered around and stared down on his lifeless body with a feeling of complete and utter shock, as their senses reeled at the terrible thing they had done.

'Huh,' muttered Pip.

They could see it was only a poor little goblin lying there.

'The poor chap has fainted,' said Pip. 'Serves him right for creeping about and frightening us all to death,' he muttered, unkindly.

The stranger suddenly stirred and opened his eyes and saw them all looking down on him. He looked terrified.

'No one is going to harm you,' said Pip, gently.

The goblin jumped to his feet. 'What's your game?' he cried gruffly. 'You have no business here.'

'I think that is what I should be asking you,' said Pip, with a suspicious look. 'Have we met before?'

There was something about the stranger he didn't trust.

'No, I don't think so,' said the naughty little goblin with a shifty look, and they all knew he was lying.

'I remember now!' cried Pip, suddenly 'You're the one that ran off with my wheelbarrow, and didn't bring it back.'

'What if I did? Do your worst! Do your worst! I would do it again if I had to!'

They glared at him.

'I have a good mind to punch your lights out,' cried Pip furiously.

'Oh, leave him alone, Pip,' cried Miranda. 'Can't you see he's suffered enough. Who cares about a stupid wheelbarrow anyway?' she muttered.

'I know it was very wrong of me,' cried the goblin. 'I stole the wheelbarrow to take my friend to hospital because he had broken his leg and was unable to walk.'

'Why didn't you say so in the first place?' muttered Pip, irritably. 'You can keep it if you want. You probably need it more than I do,' he said, generously. 'Would you mind telling us your name and what you are doing here?'

'My name is Ivan.' He suddenly burst into a loud bout of weeping. 'I've had a rotten time and I'm lucky to be alive.'

'I say, old chap, don't take on so,' said Pip kindly. 'You're safe now.'

Ivan stopped crying, blew his nose like a trumpet, dried his eyes on his red spotted handkerchief and looked around at his audience.

'I knew something was very wrong. I could feel it in the air, but I couldn't put my finger on it, until I saw all the witches in the forest.' He stared at them with a look of terror. 'There were so many of them, cackling and screeching wildly!'

They stared wordlessly back, terrified.

'They were rounding up all my friends and taking them prisoner and putting them into strange looking carts. Everyone was terrified and all the little pixies were sobbing their hearts out, and if anyone dared to defy them they beat them about the head until they were a crumbling wreck, pleading for mercy.'

'Oh, what a terrible thing to happen,' cried Pip.

'Oh, it was shocking,' cried Ivan. 'The worst nightmare anyone could ever imagine. I will never forget it as long as I live,' he sobbed bitterly. 'I don't know why the witches are here but if they don't go away, we're all going to be as dead as a plank of wood.' His eyes were red from weeping.

He stared around at them with a look of despair written all over his grumpy little face.

'I wish I'd never come here,' wailed Miranda in a baby voice.

'Oh, do shut up, Miranda,' cried Pip irritably, 'and give a chap time to think.'

'Huh, a fat lot of good that'll do. It'll need more than your brains to get us out of here!'

'I should never have brought you here,' he cried. 'You haven't got the sense you were born with and if I could turn the clock back you wouldn't be standing there.'

'It's your fault I'm here in the first place. Mr clever so and so,' she yelled back.

They went at it hammer and tongs.

'Stop it! Stop it at once!' cried Ivan. 'I've never heard anything like it in all my yesterdays. You two are supposed to be friends and not stand there arguing when all our lives are at stake.'

They stared at him.

'Oh dear, oh dear,' cried Pip, suddenly going very red in the face. 'What have I done, all this arguing is getting us nowhere. I'm sorry for my behaviour. Miranda, please forgive me. My nerves just got the better of me. It won't happen again.'

'I know how you feel,' she said. 'I'm a bag of nerves too,' she admitted. 'Sorry, Pip.'

They both smiled. And everyone calmed down. They began to talk among themselves.

'Do you remember when we played hopscotch?' asked Ivan thoughtfully.

'I remember it all too well. Why do you ask?' said Pip.

'I just thought I'd mention it. I remember another time when I did the polka dot dance with little Mercy.'

They talked about the happy times they had shared with friends.

'You talk as though this is the end,' said Pip.

'Well, isn't it?' asked Ivan, bleakly. 'We are like sitting ducks waiting to be caught. The witches can come at any time and find us here.'

Pip suddenly had a brilliant idea. 'I know what I'll do,' he cried. 'I'll go for help.'

They all stared at him in sudden hope.

'What have you got in mind, Pip?' asked Ivan, with a note of respect in his voice.

They all listened eagerly to what he had to say.

'It was a long time ago, but I remember it as clearly as if it was yesterday.'

He had their full attention.

'I had eaten juniper berries and become very ill,' explained Pip. 'I came out in a terrible rash and I couldn't stop scratching. My mouth swelled up and my lips turned blue and I knew I was dying.'

He looked around at them all.

'Then one day the wizard came to visit and he saw how ill I looked. He took me to one side and quietly worked his magic on me, and in an instant I was cured. He saved my life. As I see it,' he said thoughtfully, 'he is the only one who can save us now.'

'Do you know where he lives?' asked Ivan, looking hopeful.

'He lives in the Valley of Dreams. It is many leagues from here.' He paused for a moment. 'I wish I was more prepared.'

'I would go with you if I was strong enough,' said Ivan, with a helpless air. 'But as you can see, I'm all in.'

They had to admit it was true.

'I would be no help to you at all,' said Pansy Poppet sorrowfully. 'I would soon die of the cold. I am only a little fairy, after all, and not strong and brave like you, Pip.'

'It's the same for me,' said Tiny miserably.

They were all very sad.

Oh dear, thought Miranda. I can't let him go alone. I must help him. She took a deep breath. 'I'll go with you, Pip,' she said, and they all turned to stare at her.

'I'm not taking you,' he said.

She was furious with him. 'I'm not staying here,' she cried. 'I'm coming with you.'

'Oh, no you are not!'

'Oh, yes I am!'

They glared at one another.

'Anyone would think I was going on a little trip to the seaside instead of a dangerous journey facing life and death at every turn,' he cried angrily.

'I will never find my way home without you, Pip.'

They all stared on in dismay.

'She's got a point,' said Ivan shrewdly.

And the matter was settled.

'I wouldn't mind being a fly on the wall where those two are concerned,' said Ivan. 'There's never a dull moment.'

'You're right there,' said a voice, and they all looked around to see Theodore standing there.

'Where did you come from?' cried Pip in astonishment.

The state he was in gave them all a shock.

'What's happened to you?' cried Pip, going over to him. 'I think you had better sit down. You look terrible. Here, let me help you.' And Theodore was gently led to the nearest chair.

'It was the witches in the woods,' he cried weakly. 'They grabbed me from behind when I was out chopping wood. They forced me to eat the poison berries and left me lying there helpless and paralysed. I couldn't move a muscle.'

They stared at him in horror.

'It was all a bit of fun to them, you see. I knew I was dying when something happened,' he gasped breathlessly.

'Get him a drink of water,' said Pip, 'quickly', and Ivan rushed to do his bidding.

The woodcutter gratefully accepted the cup of water passed to him by Ivan, which he quickly gulped down.

'It was the strangest thing,' he murmured. 'I was suddenly floating above my body and saw a rainbow in the sky. I was slowly heading towards it, when I suddenly whooshed back into my body. I could move and felt quite well again. I quickly picked myself up and I ran, and ran, and ran, until I was home again, and here I am.'

'That's the strangest tale I've ever heard,' said Pip, with a puzzled look.

'I don't understand it myself.'

They didn't know what to make of it.

'Would you mind telling me what you are all doing here?'

They quickly filled him in on all the happenings that had taken place.

'It's an impossible task you've set yourselves, but I can't see any other way out. I think we should make notes,' said Theodore thoughtfully. He turned to Pip. 'Do you know the quickest route out of the forest?'

'I've been around these parts for some time but never thought of a short cut before,' he said, shaking his head.

'Can someone please get me a pen and paper out of the top drawer and I'll draw you a map.'

It was soon done. They began to get ready for the journey.

'Wrap up warmly, Miranda,' he advised. 'It's bitterly cold outside.'

It was a tearful farewell as their friends stood in the open doorway and waved them off.

Pip and Miranda set off on their long journey to save The Magic Kingdom, but time was running out…

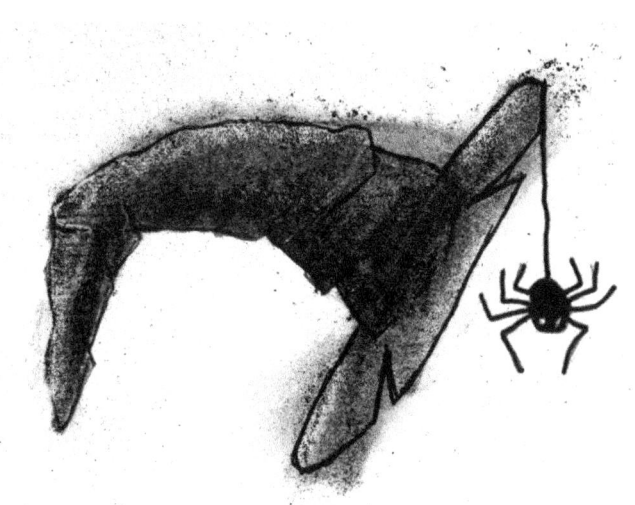

CHAPTER FOUR
THE LONG JOURNEY

As darkness fell it began to snow. They were soon in a blizzard. They were bent double against it as they struggled wearily along.

'Oh, Pip, I can't go on,' gasped Miranda. 'I must rest.'

'We must find shelter soon, Miranda,' he cried, and his voice echoed strangely against the storm.

They suddenly stumbled on a small outcrop of rock. They quickly scrambled in. It gave them shelter from the storm. The blizzard raged as they huddled close together. They were both asleep in seconds.

They woke early shivering with cold.

'It's stopped snowing,' said Pip, peering up at the grey and gloomy sky.

They could see more snow was on the way. Snow drifts were high in places.

'This is our chance,' he said. 'According to the map there is a barn not far from here.'

They scrambled out of their little shelter from the storm. It had saved both their lives.

'I'm stiff as a poker,' said Pip, suddenly stretching up.

Miranda stood quietly by watching him. 'You know what, Pip?'

He turned to look enquiringly at her.

'I get the feeling someone is spying on us.'

'I know what you mean,' he said softly. 'I did sense something similar before and put it down to my imagination.'

'It's not just me, then.'

'Let's go,' he said uneasily. His eyes searched the landscape for any other sign of life, but there was no one about.

It was a bleak and lonely place. They hurried briskly away, glancing nervously around. They had been travelling for some time when they saw the barn in the distance.

'There it is, Pip!'

'I was beginning to think we'd never find it. This map is a bit out of date,' he added. 'Hurry up, Miranda. It will be dark soon.'

They put a spurt on.

The tumbledown shack promised safe refuge for the night that was fast approaching. A dark cloud of witches could be seen in the distance flying towards them.

'The witches are coming!' shrieked Miranda, in panic.

'Run! Miranda, run!' cried Pip.

They ran into the barn breathless, and safely hidden. They peeped warily out through the slightly open door and watched the witches fly by low overhead. Their long spindly legs dangled like long black liquorice sticks as they rode their broomsticks through the darkening sky. WHOOOSH! WHOOOSH! WHOOOSH! They went on their broomsticks. It was a terrifying sight.

They were soon gone.

'They nearly caught us this time,' said Pip, closing the rickety barn door. 'Oh, Miranda!' he cried, seeing how grey she looked.

She shook like a leaf in the wind.

'You've had an awful fright. Come and sit down.' He led her to a three legged milking stool left there by someone.

Miranda quickly sat down as if her legs had turned to rubber. It wasn't long before the colour flooded back into her face.

'That's better,' said Pip. 'You had me worried there for a while.'

She gave him a troubled look. 'Sorry about that,' she said weakly. 'It was seeing the witches up close like that.'

'Nasty creatures,' he muttered, with a look of disgust.

The barn was full of straw.

Pip suddenly had a brainwave. 'Why don't we gather this lot up and make us each a bed up,' he suggested, with a wide grin. 'Then we can get a good night's rest.'

'Sounds good to me,' she said, getting up from her seat.

They began to gather up enough straw make two little beds. They were soon finished.

'That should do nicely,' said Pip with a satisfied look. 'Let's get some shut-eye before morning,' he added wisely, and Miranda agreed.

They quickly snuggled down in their straw beds like two little starlings in their nests. They were soon sleeping soundly.

Pip was suddenly wide awake. He could hear strange sounds coming from somewhere in the barn and knew they were not alone. He wondered who was out there and knew he would have to go and investigate. Miranda was sleeping soundly beside him and he decided not to wake her. He would handle this alone.

He climbed out of his nice warm bed as silently as a panther and went to investigate. He stumbled about in the dark then bumped into an old wheelbarrow that someone had left there. His little heart was beating like a drum as he made his way around it, and tripped over a brush shank that had been propped up against the barn wall. He fell headlong to the floor with the most awful racket of clattering tools and farm implements falling on top of him.

It was loud enough to wake the dead.

The noise woke Miranda. She looked wildly around for Pip, and saw his empty bed. Pip had deserted her. She was terrified as she stared around at the ghostly monsters reflected on the walls by the moonlight streaming in through a small hole in the roof. She felt so alone.

It was the middle of the night.

Pip suddenly saw a dark shadow heading towards him and he was paralysed with fear and couldn't move an inch.

'Who is there?' barked a voice. 'Own up, whoever you are.'

'Foxy! Is that you?' cried Pip, in astonishment.

'What is the meaning of this, Pip?' shouted Foxy furiously. 'You woke me from a lovely dream I was having, not to mention scaring me half to death with all the noise you were making.'

'Oh, Foxy,' Pip said, picking himself up off the floor. 'You scared the living daylights out of me!'

'Huh,' said Foxy. 'Serves you right, creeping around like a burglar in the middle of the night.'

'Oh, Foxy, I'm awfully sorry, but you could have been anybody.'

'I understand completely. Now would you mind telling me what you are doing here?' He suddenly sniffed the air. 'Who else here is here with you, Pip?'

'Only Miranda. You must come and meet her, Foxy, I'm sure you will like her.'

They made their way over to Miranda. They got the fright of their lives when they suddenly saw her standing there with a pitchfork held up for protection.

'It's only me, Miranda,' shouted Pip urgently, before any harm was done. 'Look, I've brought my friend Foxy to meet you.'

'I won't harm you, my dear,' said Foxy, warily.

Miranda could see a very handsome fox standing beside Pip. 'How dare you sneak off like that without telling me where you're going!' she cried angrily. Then all the fight seemed to go out of her. 'Oh, Pip, I thought you had left me and I was never going to see you ever again.'

He could still see the terror in her eyes.

'Oh, Miranda, I'm sorry for leaving you, but I thought it was for the best. I had to find out who else was in the barn and if we were in any danger. Do please forgive me and I promise you, hand on heart,' – he placed both hands on his fast beating heart – 'it will never happen again.'

She flung the pitchfork down onto the ground. 'It had better not,' she said, a little shakily, now all the fight had gone out of her.

'A promise made is a promise kept,' he said solemnly.

She smiled weakly at him. 'I forgive you, Pip.'

They were friends once more.

'Come and meet an old friend of mine.'

Foxy and Miranda were properly introduced.

'She is an attractive little creature, isn't she,' he remarked pleasantly.

They talked well into the early hours until Pip wisely suggested they try to get a few hours' sleep. They quickly snuggled down into their straw beds once more.

They were soon sleeping soundly.

They woke early and were talking in low voices when Pip suddenly put a finger to his lips. 'Shush,' he warned. 'There is a stranger among us, and he knows we are here.'

Oh, no, here we go again, thought Miranda, suddenly frightened.

They strained their ears and could just hear a strange scrabbling noise coming from somewhere above their heads. They felt their insides wobble with fear. They craned their necks to look up.

'You had better come out if you know what's good for you,' shouted Pip bravely, ready to face whoever was up there.

'I need help, not to be bullied by the likes of you,' screeched a barn owl. 'I am trapped up here. Well, don't just stand there gawping. Are you going to help me or not?'

'I suppose I had better go and rescue him,' said Pip, beginning to look for a long ladder.

He soon found one propped up against the wall. It was very old and the wood was rotten in places. He placed it carefully in position. Miranda held the ladder steady for him as he began to climb up it.

'Oh, Pip, please be careful you don't fall.'

He was glad to reach the top and quickly stepped off the ladder and straight onto the wooden beams that crisscrossed the roof of the barn. He saw at once where the problem lay. The barn owl had become tangled up in chicken wire and the more he struggled the tighter it became. It was wrapped around his neck and he was slowly choking to death.

'You took your time, I must say,' screeched the barn owl.

'You must keep very still while I cut you free,' said Pip, taking out his little penknife that he kept for emergencies.

He began to cut away at the chicken wire until the barn owl was released and could finally breathe properly once more.

'Thanks, mate,' he squawked, and quickly flew down to join the others.

Pip turned back to the ladder and began his slow descent of the very unsafe ladder that threatened to break at any time. He gave a huge sigh of relief as soon as his feet touched the ground.

He could hear shouting. The barn owl was in a very bad mood.

'You lazy lot of layabouts, I could have died up there!'

'Just who do you think you are talking to?' demanded Miranda. 'Old bossy boots,' she muttered.

'For your information, my name is Mr Hoot,' he squawked indignantly.

'You ungrateful wretch,' cried Foxy, looking very annoyed. 'Pip has just risked his life to save you.'

Pip was astonished. 'What on earth is going on here?' he demanded angrily.

The barn owl suddenly looked ashamed of himself. 'I'm sorry,' he cried weakly. 'I should never have behaved like that. Do please forgive me.' He gazed at them with bleary eyes and didn't look at all well. 'I haven't eaten for some time now,' he grumbled.

He told them how he had been unable to hunt for food and had almost frozen to death the last time he was out. He had been trapped for some time and was as thin as a rake and dying of starvation. They soon forgave him for being so bad tempered when they realised the state he was in.

'Why didn't you call out last night?' enquired Pip. 'You must have heard the awful noise I made.'

'I was afraid,' admitted Mr Hoot.

'I'm going to look outside,' said Pip suddenly.

He went over to the barn door and pushed and shoved but it wouldn't budge. It was frozen solid. They all surged forward to lend a hand; they put their weight against it until it opened wide enough for them all to see outside.

A chill blast of cold air rushed in.

CHAPTER FIVE
THE ICY KINGDOM

They looked out on an icy kingdom. Everything was frozen into stillness.

'This is the end for all of us,' cried Pip loudly. 'We are trapped here.'

'I wish I'd never come here!' wailed Miranda loudly. 'I want to go home.'

'My dear child, don't take on so,' said Mr Hoot, looking very upset.

'It's like the end of the world,' said Foxy, looking stunned. 'We are all going to die here.'

'Shut your big mouth,' cried Mr Hoot, giving Foxy an angry glare.

'I'm not standing here to be spoken to like that!'

They hurried back inside and quickly shut the door behind them. They were all terrified.

'There must be a way out of this mess,' said Pip, staring at the ground with a hopeless air about him.

'It's like a nightmare.' Foxy howled loudly, and they all told him to shut up.

'Must you be so dramatic?' squawked Mr Hoot belligerently.

The fear and tension in the air soon had them arguing and squabbling among themselves.

'This is the end for all of us,' squawked Mr Hoot, flapping his wings dramatically.

'I have a good mind to slap your wings,' cried Foxy angrily. 'Can't you see she's upset?'

'There is no need to speak to him like that,' said Pip, looking annoyed.

'Oh dear,' said Mr Hoot, 'all this bickering is getting us nowhere.'

'Oh, shut up, the lot of you,' cried Miranda angrily, 'and let me think.'

They were all too shocked to speak.

'I have an idea,' she said thoughtfully. 'You know all those farm implements that are lying around, do you think you could use them to make snow shoes out of all the bits of wood lying around?'

They stared at her in admiration.

'I have a better idea,' said Pip, suddenly jumping up and looking very excited about something.

They went over to inspect the materials lying around and soon discovered enough wood to make a sledge big enough for all of them to ride in. They set to work hammering and knocking busily away. They soon had it finished. They stood back to admire their handiwork.

'I say,' said Pip proudly. 'That is a little beauty and no mistake.'

'Wow, isn't it super,' said Foxy.

'It is a fine piece of craftsmanship, if I may say so,' said Mr Hoot.

'Let's see if it's any good,' said Miranda, eager to try it out.

They dragged the sledge outside and soon had it facing down the steep slope.

'Get in, everyone, and I will push us off,' cried Pip bossily.

They all scrambled in. There was plenty of room.

'Hold tight,' he cried, and with one gentle push the sledge began to slide slowly forward. He quickly jumped in and joined the others.

'Oh, bravo, well done!' they chorused.

The sledge soon gathered speed. Faster and faster it went until they were soon whizzing along at great speed. The scenery passed by in a blur as they shot downhill with all the speed of an express train.

'Yippee!' cried Pip joyfully, and everyone began to join in.

'Yippee! Yippee!' they all shouted gleefully.

They were enjoying themselves so much.

A huge mountain came into view. It was directly in their path and they were headed straight for it. They were going to crash into it. They were going too fast to jump out. Their faces were frozen with fear. They watched helplessly as it drew near.

'Hold on tight,' cried Pip, grim faced. 'We might come out of this alive.'

But it seemed hopeless.

A door in the mountain suddenly opened up and they whooshed straight in with all the speed of an arrow. The sledge slowed down and finally came to a halt just inside the entrance. They were inside the biggest mountain they had ever seen. They all climbed out looking badly shaken.

A mighty explosion could be heard in the distance, making them glance fearfully around. A figure came hurrying towards them. He looked every inch as though he was enjoying himself.

'Ha, so you have arrived,' he said, chuckling. 'I've just blown up the witches that were following you.'

They stared at him in amazement.

'Oh, yes,' he said, 'they were on your tail. That was a brilliant idea making a sledge. It saved your lives.' He rubbed his hands gleefully together. 'It was lucky for you I saw you coming through my telescope.'

'That explains it,' said Pip, smiling. 'We are very grateful to you for saving our lives.'

'The witches are everywhere, you know.' The figure scowled fiercely. I'd like to get my hands around their scrawny little necks and squeeze the life out of them until they beg for mercy,' he muttered bitterly.

'You have no idea the trouble they have caused.'

They stared at him curiously.

'You must be wondering who I am,' he said, with a twinkle in his eye. 'I am Alphonse, guardian of the secret worlds, and you are?'

They quickly introduced themselves.

'I must say I am very surprised to see you all,' said Alphonse. 'Would you mind telling me where you are going?'

Pip spoke up. 'We need the wizard's help to save The Magic Kingdom.'

'I'm afraid that's not possible.'

They stared at him in horror.

'He's gone to toy land to mend all the broken, unloved toys that some naughty children have thrown away instead of giving them to someone else in need who would love and care for them,' said Alphonse, sadly shaking his head, and his long white beard waved to and fro like a flag in the wind.

Miranda stared at him, fascinated.

'This is the end,' cried Pip mournfully. 'We'll never save The Magic Kingdom now.' Pip buried his face in his hands in despair.

They were all very frightened.

'I say, old chap, don't take on so,' said Alphonse, deeply moved. He stroked his long white beard thoughtfully. 'There is someone you must meet.'

They looked at Alphonse shrouded in mystery.

'The witches will get their come-uppance and we will be rid of them forever.' He gleefully rubbed his hands together.

They stared at him as if he'd suddenly gone mad.

'You must have an audience with the King and Queen of Fairyland,' he announced grandly. 'They will be able to help you, or I'll eat my hat.'

'Can you show me the way?' Pip was suddenly filled with hope.

'Aha,' said Alphonse triumphantly. 'Come with me.' He hurried away.

They quickly ran after him.

Alphonse led the way, his bright red cloak flowing wildly out behind him. The inside of the mountain was lit up like a Christmas tree: millions of crystals sparkled and shone out from every nook and cranny in the rock face. It was a secret place they were in. They stopped in front of a large oak door with strange carvings of flying creatures long since gone.

'Here we are,' said Alphonse, fumbling for a set of keys tied securely around his waist.

He inserted the key in the lock and threw open the door, quickly ushering them in. They entered a garden of such wondrous beauty it took their breath away. The scent of roses filled the air and wild and wonderful flowers grew in gay profusion everywhere they looked.

The sun shone brightly down from a cloudless blue sky and butterflies flew from flower to flower, and even the little birds chirped merrily in the trees. A marble statue of a magnificent flying horse stood in the centre of the garden for all to see. Alphonse whistled softly, and to their amazement the flying horse suddenly came to life, whinnied softly and came trotting over to them.

'There, there, my beauty,' murmured Alphonse, tenderly stroking him.

It was plain to see they were old friends.

'His name is Pegasus,' said Alphonse, with a look of pride. 'He is the last of his kind. He is the stuff that dreams are made of,' he added, smiling.

It was the most amazing sight they had ever seen and they stared dumbfounded.

'Pegasus is the only one who can take you to the Fairy Kingdom. Without him you will never find it,' said Alphonse softly. 'It's been a well kept secret for centuries and can only to be revealed in times of great danger.' He paused. 'I think we can safely say that that time is here. Pegasus will fly again.'

'Do you mean I am to ride him?' cried Pip, with a feeling of awe.

'Can I go with Pip?' said Miranda, her eyes shining with excitement.

They both looked hopefully at Alphonse.

He stroked his long white beard. 'I don't see why not. After all, you are here and I suppose there must be a very good reason for it. I will look after your friends,' he added, smiling at Foxy and Mr Hoot standing nearby.

They were very pleased to be staying behind. They'd had enough adventures to last them a lifetime. Pip and Miranda were soon astride Pegasus.

'Hold on tight,' cried Pip, as Miranda wrapped her arms around his waist so she wouldn't fall off.

Alphonse gave Pegasus a sound slap on his rear. 'Off you go, my beauty,' he cried.

Pegasus leapt high into the air and they were off. Alphonse, Foxy and Mr Hoot watched them fly high into the sky. Pegasus flew higher and higher, until the ground beneath them had disappeared.

It was a magical journey.

'Oh, Pip, this is wonderful,' cried Miranda, laughing.

CHAPTER SIX
PEGASUS FLIES AGAIN

'Gosh, this is exciting,' cried Pip, his hair blowing in the wind.

They could see in the distance a little castle with twinkling lights all around it. They were flying steadily towards it when suddenly a loud clap of thunder was heard and the sky went very dark. They looked back and saw a group of flying witches sneaking up behind them.

'Oh, Pip what are we going to do?' cried Miranda. 'They mustn't catch us.'

'I'm sure we are safe from harm,' he said doubtfully.

They suddenly disappeared into a strange mist.

'Don't worry, Miranda, nothing can catch us now,' he cried, laughing.

Their journey was soon over and they wisely dismounted. They were in the castle grounds. They were quickly surrounded by soldiers pointing their guns at them in a threatening manner. A figure came hurrying towards them. He looked very important and wore a chain of office around his neck.

'You must be Pip, and you are Miranda. It is a pleasure to meet you both.'

Their faces flushed with surprise.

'I am known as Aldo,' he boomed in a very loud voice. He ordered the soldiers to stand back. 'You will not be needed,' he said. 'I will deal with this.'

They replaced their guns on their shoulders and briskly marched away with military precision. Pegasus was gently led away.

'I know why you are here,' Aldo said, turning back to face Pip and Miranda. 'There is much to discuss. Please come this way.' He turned and walked briskly away.

Pip and Miranda silently followed him with curious looks thrown at one another. The feelings of being in a huge castle with high domed ceilings that looked out on a million stars twinkling down on them as they walked briskly along were magical. They stopped in front of a huge oak door. Two sentries stood on duty at the door. Their guns were raised in a threatening manner.

'Halt! Who goes there?' called a sentry.

'It is I, Aldo, the Queen's consort. Please let us pass.'

They were immediately allowed entry.

Pip and Miranda were astonished to see the room was full of fairy folk. They were all talking quietly together. Their little troubled faces turned to watch the strangers as they passed them by. Not a sound was to be heard.

They had entered the throne room. The King and Queen of Fairyland were dressed in shimmering robes and seated on golden thrones. They observed the trio as they approached. Aldo bowed low and so did Pip. Miranda curtsied prettily.

'Our visitors have arrived, Your Majesty,' announced Aldo, with great ceremony.

'I can see that,' said the King, with a troubled look. 'So this is Pip, and you must be Miranda.'

They both looked startled.

'You have done well to have made it this far,' said the King. 'What can I do for you?'

Pip suddenly spoke up. 'We are in a desperate situation and we have come to you for help, Your Majesty.'

'We know all about you. We have been watching your progress on the screen,' he explained. 'These are terrible times, Pip. Come, there is something you must see before any more words can be said.' The King stepped down from his throne with great pomp and ceremony. 'Come, my dear,' he held out his hand and it was gently taken by the delicate hand of his queen.

They entered the picture house. A great cinema screen covered one wall.

They took their seats. Pip and Miranda were allowed to sit beside the King and Queen as special guests.

It was a huge honour.

The picture house quickly filled up as everyone poured silently in after them and only the shuffling of feet could be heard as they took their seats and no one spoke. There was a sense of urgency in the air. They waited until everyone was seated. The lights were dimmed. The cinema screen was switched on.

They watched as the film began to roll.

It showed The Magic Kingdom with lush green valleys and forests and flowers in bud. The scenery was breathtaking. There was happiness and laughter everywhere. They watched the fairy folk who lived there going about their daily chores and children playing. Then slowly it began to change, and suddenly everything was barren and bleak. Witches could be seen rounding everyone up. They were herded into strange looking vehicles and taken to the witches' castle, high on a hill in a strange land far, far away, and thrown into the deepest dungeon.

There was no one left and the world had changed dramatically from what it had once been. A grey mist covered the whole of the countryside and a chill winter frost began to creep over every living thing, until all that could be seen was ice and mist. The cinema screen went blank. It was the end.

There was a stunned silence.

'I have never seen anything so cruel in all my born days.' Pip was horrified. 'I see it all now.'

Miranda was very upset and tried not to show it by bursting into tears.

'Now you understand what we are up against. We will retire to the throne room and discuss this further,' said the King, rising from his seat and taking the hand of his queen. They left the picture house.

Pip and Miranda followed them out with heads bowed in sadness. Everyone was very unhappy as they silently shuffled out. The throne room was entered with great ceremony. Pip and Miranda stood before the King and Queen, once more seated on their thrones.

'I don't understand,' said Pip. 'Why is this happening? What is it the witches want, Your Majesty?'

'The Queen of Witches wants the secret to eternal youth,' explained the King, with a look of contempt.

'Well, I'll eat my gum boots – so that's the answer,' muttered Pip.

'All a witch has to do is drink the water,' said the Queen, 'and as you know, Pip, witches never drink water. For some strange reason they seem to be afraid of it.'

'Are you telling me that all a witch has to do is drink the water?' exclaimed Pip, incredulously. 'Well, I never,' he said. 'And to think the witches have turned all the water into ice, and not a drop to drink anywhere.' He shook his head in disbelief. 'So that's what it's all about.'

'What I don't understand,' piped up Miranda, 'is why didn't anyone just give them what they wanted? It's only water after all!'

'You tell them, my dear,' said the King, with a deeply troubled look, and anyone could see his heart was breaking.

'We didn't know the witches had invaded The Magic Kingdom until it was too late to come to its rescue,' explained the little fairy queen. 'The secret to eternal youth is only known to those who live here in the kingdom of Fairyland. There is only one other person who knows the secret to eternal youth and that is the wizard.' She paused and looked at Pip. 'I know you tried to find him.'

'Yes, Your Majesty,' said Pip quietly.

'We had no idea what had happened until we saw you both on the screen.' She looked as if she was about to cry. 'You were both so brave.' She paused for a moment. 'Anyone from Fairyland entering The Magic Kingdom as it is now would die instantly of the cold. So you see, my dears, all we can do is stand helplessly by and do nothing.'

She looked despairingly at them.

'We need a warrior to take a bottle of water to the Queen of Witches in return for freedom for The Magic Kingdom,' said the King. 'Until they get what they want they will never leave it.

I'm not much to look at, thought Pip, but I'm sure I could do it. 'I'll take it to her, Your Majesty,' said Pip firmly.

They all stared at him wide-eyed.

The King was astounded at his bravery. 'You will be risking your life.'

'They are my friends too,' he cried. 'And I can't just sit around and do nothing, waiting for them to die. I must try to save them.'

'I can see that your mind is made up,' said the King.' He turned to Aldo. 'See that he has everything he will need for the journey.'

Aldo jumped to do his bidding. 'At once, my King,' he said.

Pip was given his instructions and several items he would need for the journey. A small child-like pixie dashed away to get the water. He was back in an instant carrying the bottle of precious liquid in a small blue bottle to disguise what it really was. He handed it to Aldo, who gently took it from him.

'Guard it with your life,' he said, passing it over to Pip, and Pip quickly put it into his bag for safe keeping.

'Once you are inside the witches' castle you must be very brave and stand your ground. Demand to see the Queen of Witches and get her promise to leave The Magic Kingdom before any transaction takes place,' said Aldo, trembling. He gave him a warning. 'Beware of her, Pip, she is more dangerous than a coiled snake.' His voice faltered a little. 'I think that's everything. You know what you must do.'

'A word of advice, Pip,' said the King worriedly. 'Never turn your back on a witch, or you won't live to tell the tale.'

It was a warning that Pip took to heart.

'You would have been captured too, Pip, if you hadn't gone on one of your little adventures into the world of humans,' said the little queen, with a knowing look.

'I know,' he said thoughtfully. 'I realised that some time ago, Your Majesty.'

'You are a courageous little elf, Pip,' said the Queen. Unshed tears sparkled on her long eyelashes.

It nearly broke Pip's little heart to see her looking so unhappy.

'Oh, yes, indeed,' said the King. 'Your name will go down in the history books as the bravest little elf of all time.'

Suddenly cheering and clapping broke out. Pip looked bashful at all the praise he was receiving.

Miranda was grinning at him. 'You'll be getting too big for your boots if this keeps up,' she said.

'You can't talk to a warrior like that,' he said, with a huge grin.

'I see Pip has met his match there,' someone said.

There were nods and secret smiles.

'She's awfully pretty,' said a little fairy admiringly. 'Her hair is quite the loveliest colour of chestnut brown I've ever seen.'

It was time to leave.

They were soon outside in the courtyard and they could see the little red helicopter waiting for them. They quickly jumped in. The pilot started the engine and they were off flying high into the sky.

The moon smiled down on them. 'Good luck,' she whispered.

They travelled all through the night, and it was early morning when they landed safely back in The Magic Kingdom. They quickly jumped out and ran to the trees for cover. The pilot started up the engine again and gave them a brief wave.

'Good luck,' he called, as he flew high into the sky on his way home.

They set off on their journey to the witches' castle. They had travelled quite a distance through the bitterly cold weather when they spotted something moving swiftly along the skyline a little to one side. They stared at it with frightening intensity.

'What do you think it is, Pip?' said Miranda, with a tremor in her voice.

'I don't know but I think we are just about to find out.' He held the telescope to his eye and looked through it. 'Why, bless my woolly jumper, if it isn't Princess Aurora! Quick, Miranda, we must attract her attention.'

They waved madly.

Miranda took off her long woolly scarf and began waving it in the air as hard as she could. The snowmobile turned in their direction.

'She has seen us and is coming this way,' he cried excitedly.

They waited for her to approach.

She stopped in front of them. 'Quick, hop aboard,' she cried urgently, 'before we are seen.'

They quickly jumped in and were soon speeding away. They came to a cave in the forest. It was well hidden. They quickly whizzed inside and stopped inside a huge underground cavern.

'You can get out now,' cried Princess Aurora. 'We are safe here.'

They quickly climbed out of the vehicle and looked around them in astonishment at the little elves, pixies, dwarves and goblins that belonged to that land. They were all huddled together looking terrified. They were hiding from the witches.

'I suppose you've got a tale to tell,' said Princess Aurora shrewdly.

'We have,' said Pip, looking grim.

They all crowded around to hear what he had to say.

Pip explained everything in great detail. 'And time is running out...' he cried urgently. 'And we still have a long way to go.'

Everyone was astonished. They stared at them in awe.

'Well, I must say,' exclaimed one little gnome with a wide-eyed expression. 'I've heard everything now.'

'They are very brave,' mumbled a voice in the crowd.

'They deserve a medal,' said another voice at the back. And everyone agreed wholeheartedly.

'I can take you part of the way,' said Princess Aurora. 'We had better leave at once, before darkness falls.'

They were grateful for the ride. They quickly climbed aboard, and before you could say Pumpkin Pie they were up and away. They were speeding along when suddenly the snowmobile crashed into a spike sticking out of the ground.

They were all thrown wildly out as it turned over.

'Is anyone hurt?' cried Pip, quickly getting to his feet.

'No, I don't think so,' said Miranda, shakily, rubbing her elbow.

'We're lucky no one was killed,' said Princess Aurora.

The snowmobile lay on its side. They went over to inspect it. They stared miserably down at it.

'Let's push it upright then we can see what the damage is,' said Pip, glowering at it.

They soon had it upright. They were all very pleased to see it was still in good working order. It only had a few scratches on the silver paintwork.

'It could have been a lot worse,' said Princess Aurora.

They all agreed they'd had a lucky escape.

The way ahead was treacherous. The path was strewn with rocks, stones and boulders, and impossible to negotiate with the wonderful snowmobile.

'We can't go on, I'm afraid, it is far too dangerous,' said the princess.

'We are grateful for the help you have given us in bringing us this far,' said Pip.

'I feel as if I have always known you,' said Miranda suddenly. 'And,' she added thoughtfully, 'you remind me of Aunty Jane – she is always helping people too.'

Princess Aurora reached into a little pouch that hung from a golden belt around her waist and took out two pink candy bars. She gave them one each. 'This will lighten your burden.'

They each took one with wide smiles, and thanked her for her kindness.

'This is goodbye then,' she said, as she climbed back into her snowmobile. It skimmed over the ice and snow until she was a little dot in the distance, then she was gone.

They were sorry to see her go.

'I'm going to eat mine now,' said Miranda, taking off the wrapper.

'So am I,' said Pip, and took a big bite. 'Scrumptious,' he said, munching happily away.

'It's the most delicious thing I've ever tasted, Pip.'

They began to walk along, feeling as though they hadn't a care in the world, instead of being troubled by all the danger that lay ahead. As they bit into the candy bar the magic began to do its work.

CHAPTER SEVEN
THEY RUN FOR THEIR LIVES

'The witches are coming! Run! Miranda, run!'

They raced for the woods and were quickly hidden. The witches were flying through the darkening sky low overhead and they were in danger of being seen. WHOOOSH! WHOOOSH! WHOOOSH! It was a dreadful sound they made on their broomsticks.

Pip and Miranda stayed hidden until they had gone.

'That's the last we'll see of them,' said Pip, climbing out from behind the bushes with Miranda close behind him.

They hurried along, still trembling with fear as they scanned the grey and gloomy sky for any witches that might suddenly appear. They saw something moving along the ground in front of them. It was partially covered in a white coating of snow and they couldn't make it out.

But it was big.

'That's no mouse,' Pip said in a whisper.

'Oh, Pip, what are we going to do?' whispered Miranda.

They were glued to the spot with fear.

'Go and hide, Miranda, and leave this to me,' he whispered.

She gave him a terrified look before running to hide behind the nearest tree. She peeped warily out. Pip waited until she was safely hidden before scraping up enough snow to make a snowball, and all the time the enemy drew closer. He took aim and threw the snowball at the unsuspecting victim. Then quick as a flash he dropped out of sight.

'Ouch, that hurt,' cried an angry voice. A huge white fluffy bunny rabbit popped his head up out of the snow and glared furiously around.

Miranda gasped in surprise when she saw it, and stepped out from behind the tree. 'I don't believe it,' she cried. 'It's a white angora rabbit! Oh, isn't he adorable!'

'Rabbit Ears!' cried Pip in astonishment, coming forward. 'What are you doing here?'

'Is that you, Pip?' the rabbit cried angrily. 'I do believe you have just belted me with a snowball. And you call yourself a friend!'

'Oh, Rabbit Ears, do please forgive me. I had no idea it was you or I would never have thrown it. You gave me an awful fright, you know,' he admitted sheepishly.

'Did I really?' Rabbit Ears said in surprise.

'It's good to see you, old friend. May I ask what you are doing here, so far from home?'

'I might ask you the same, Pip,' said Rabbit Ears. 'I'm looking for my daughter Esmeralda. The naughty little minx has wandered off again and I can't find her anywhere. I will have to return to my burrow and hope she has found her way home.' He looked at Miranda with interest. 'Who is that delightful creature standing beside you, Pip?'

'Oh, you mean Miranda,' cried Pip, laughing. Miranda couldn't help smiling.

They were quickly introduced.

'It's very nice to meet you, my dear,' said Rabbit Ears warmly. 'Would you care to tell me what you are both doing here?'

Pip told him all about their journey and the witches. He left nothing out.

'These are terrible times, Pip. You must allow me to help you. Jump on my back and I will give you the ride of your life.'

'Oh, Rabbit Ears, how marvellous,' cried Miranda.

'A marvellous offer,' agreed Pip, grinning from ear to ear.

They were soon comfortably settled on the big broad back.

'Hold on tight,' cried Rabbit Ears, giving a mighty leap up into the air; they were off.

They bounded over the snow in great leaps and bounds, until they had covered a great distance in a very short time. He stopped suddenly and they went flying over his head to land flat out in the snow. They struggled to their feet laughing.

'Whoops-a-daisy!' cried Rabbit Ears. 'That was clumsy of me!'

'Oh, Rabbit Ears, that was wonderful,' cried Miranda, brushing the snow from her clothes. 'I'd like to do that again some time.' She chortled with glee.

'Fantastic!' said Pip, chuckling.

They fell about laughing.

'Glad to oblige,' said Rabbit Ears, wondering what all the fuss was about. He couldn't see anything funny about landing in cold wet snow. 'I must leave you here. Goodbye, dear friends,' he said, before bounding away.

'Goodbye. Goodbye,' they cried.

He was soon lost to sight.

They travelled on until they came to a very dangerous place. The uneven ground was scattered with huge boulders poking up out of the ground like big broken teeth, and potholes the size of saucepans.

'I don't like this place at all,' said Pip worriedly. 'We must take tremendous care walking through here.'

'I can see that,' Miranda said.

They set off cautiously. They were making steady progress when they heard a tremendous roar.

'What's making that awful noise, Pip?'

'If I'm not mistaken, that sounds like someone is in trouble,' said Pip. 'C'mon, let's take a look.'

'If you say so,' she said, reluctantly.

'Whatever it is out there is in a great deal of pain and maybe we can help.'

They headed to where the sound was coming from and saw a huge bear standing all alone in the wilderness. They were out in the open, standing in plain view. The bear saw them and let out a mighty roar that was terrifying to hear. They turned to run for their lives when they heard him cry out.

'Oh, please don't leave me here to die,' he cried. 'I can't move. My leg is caught in a trap. Boohoo,' he cried loudly. 'Boohoo. I'm in terrible pain.'

They hurried over to him in alarm. They could see at once where the trouble lay. The bear had his leg caught in the steel jaws of a trap. They were both horrified at what they saw.

'Steady on, old chap, we are here to help you,' said Pip, adding cautiously, 'Stand still and don't move.' He bent down to take a closer look. 'I will need your help here, Miranda.'

'What do you want me to do, Pip?'

They were both low to the ground.

'Be ready to lift his leg out when I say the word.'

'Just tell me when.' Miranda watched as Pip prised open the heavy steel jaws, wider and wider, until they were wide apart.

'Now, Miranda, now!' he cried. 'Lift the leg out!'

Miranda gently lifted it out of the steel jaws. As soon as it was clear, Pip let go the trap and jumped back as the steel teeth clanged viciously shut.

It made them both jump.

Pip inspected the wound. 'I must say, you are very fortunate to have no broken bones.' He looked up at the big bear with the gentle brown eyes.

'Oh, how clever you are,' cried the bear. 'You have repaid me with kindness and saved my life. Please tell me your names?'

'I'm known as Pip, and this is my friend Miranda.'

They smiled up at him.

'I am Teddy Bear.'

It wasn't long before they were chatting away like old friends. Suddenly they were startled to hear a clap of thunder and an avalanche of snow came hurtling towards them. They suddenly all took off as though the devil himself was after them. They didn't look back until they were safely away. They all knew they'd had a narrow escape.

'That'll be the witches up to their nasty tricks again,' said Pip in disgust. 'I wouldn't be surprised if they are hiding somewhere.'

Miranda gave a terrified look over her shoulder. There were too many hidey holes scattered about for her liking.

'Let's get away from here,' said Pip urgently.

They quickly left.

'Would you mind telling me where you are bound for?' asked Teddy in his soft gruff voice.

'No, I don't mind at all,' said Pip, glancing up at him. 'You'll give me a stiff neck,' he said, chuckling. 'We are on our way to the witches' castle with a bottle of the precious water to gain our freedom.'

He told Teddy all about their journey and the witches. He left nothing out.

'I'm glad I'm not in your shoes,' said Teddy gruffly. 'I wouldn't have your courage to attempt such a thing.'

Miranda tripped and fell.

Pip quickly came to her aid and helped her to her feet, but as soon as she tried to stand up, she cried out in agony. 'Oh, Pip, I've hurt my ankle.'

He helped balance her against a big stone, so she could take her weight off her foot.

'Let me take a look,' he said, bending over it. He gently felt all around it. 'It's a bad sprain, I'm afraid. You won't be walking on that for a while.'

'Oh, Pip, you must go on,' she cried, her face twisted in pain.

'I will do no such thing,' he said, with a note of horror in his voice at the very idea.

'You must leave me here,' she insisted.

'I can't leave you here and just walk away,' he cried indignantly. 'We must rest here until your ankle is better.'

'But what about The Magic Kingdom? We'll never be able to save it now,' she cried bitterly.

Pip's face was a picture of despair.

Teddy had been standing by watching and wondered if there was anything he could do to help them when an extraordinary thing happened. An idea suddenly popped into his head, as though someone had put it there.

'Jump on my back,' he cried, 'and I will take you there.'

He took them both by surprise.

'Do you really mean it?' cried Pip excitedly.

'You would do that for us?' exclaimed Miranda.

'You need help and I am here,' said Teddy, suddenly crouching down on all fours to make it easier for them to climb up onto his big broad back.

'Here, take my arm, Miranda,' suggested Pip, 'and I will help you up, that is, if Teddy doesn't mind bending a little closer to the ground.'

'Will this do?' he asked gruffly, lowering himself low to the ground.

'Oh, Teddy, you are kind,' said Miranda, heaving herself up onto his back with the help of Pip.

As soon as she was safely settled, Pip took a flying leap up beside her.

They snuggled down together into the deep warm fur.

'Nice and comfy?' murmured Teddy, before he ambled off.

It was very comfortable on the bear's back, and the gentle rocking motion soon had them fast asleep.

CHAPTER EIGHT
THE KINGDOM OF WITCHES

They woke from a deep refreshing sleep. They could just see in the distance the witches' castle. It stood out on the skyline, dark and threatening. The mountains lay dead ahead.

'Our journey will soon be over,' said Pip, with a sense of dread. 'You can tell it's full of evil just by looking at it.'

'Oh, Pip, I wish we didn't have to go there.'

'You don't have to do this, you know. I can always go on alone.'

'I'm not leaving you now,' she said.

'I never thought I would say this, but have you any idea how much help you have given me already? So don't feel that you have to come with me now.'

'That's what friends are for.'

'You have turned out to be a true friend,' he said.

They soon came to a standstill. They had arrived and could go no further. The high mountains surrounded them.

'I think our ride is over,' said Pip. 'We'll climb down, Teddy, if you don't mind letting us off now.'

'Certainly,' said Teddy.

Pip quickly jumped down from Teddy's back. He turned to help Miranda. She leaned heavily on Pip as she reached the ground. He looked worriedly on as she tried out her injured ankle by putting her weight on it. She was soon standing upright.

She gave a cry of delight. 'Oh, it's better, Pip!' She turned to Teddy. 'I'm lucky to have you for a friend.'

Pip looked up into a pair of gentle brown eyes. 'My dear friend,' he said. 'We owe our lives to you. Your kindness will never be forgotten.' He bowed gallantly.

'Tush, was nothing,' Teddy said shyly.

The mountains were all around them. They rose up as high as the sky. They were covered in an icy coating as clear as glass, impossible to climb and blocking the way ahead.

'There is no way through,' cried Pip, with a note of desperation in his voice.

They searched in vain.

'Have we come all this way for nothing?' wailed Miranda.

They were filled with despair.

'I know a secret way in,' said Teddy.

They stared at him in amazement.

'Come on, I'll show you.'

They followed him to the entrance of a cave.

'This is our escape route,' said Pip, grinning gleefully.

'I remember playing here with my friends when I was a baby bear,' said Teddy. 'We stumbled on the tunnel quite by chance. It was all very exciting in those days. We weren't afraid of anything. We went gaily through the tunnel and came out the other side and saw the witches, all huddled together chanting. Oh, it was an awful sight. I shall never forget it as long as I live.'

They stared up at him speechless with fear in their hearts.

'We dashed back into the tunnel before we were seen. We didn't stop running until we were safely home. They robbed us of our childhood and we never went there again. I had almost forgotten the tunnel was there,' he added thoughtfully.

He looked sadly down on them from his great height. They looked so small and defenceless in his eyes.

It was time to leave.

'Go and hide,' said Miranda worriedly.

They both knew the witches would roast him on a fire and eat him for their supper if he was captured.

'When this is all over, we will hold the biggest party you have ever seen, and that's a promise,' said Pip firmly.

'I will look forward to it.'

He hurried quickly away.

'I hope he's going to be all right, Pip.'

'Don't worry about him, Miranda. He is the biggest bear I have ever seen. His size alone would frighten anybody off!'

Looks can be deceiving, she thought to herself. He was a big softie really.

The sky went black.

They looked up and saw it was full of witches, far too many to count. They were all racing towards the castle on broomsticks. Pip and Miranda ran into the tunnel and quickly hid. They peeped out of their secret hideaway to watch the witches fly by in their hundreds. They were both filled with horror.

Pip suddenly remembered it was the night of the full moon, a time of great evil when witches were at their most powerful. He decided to remain silent and not tell Miranda. He didn't want to add to her fears.

The sky was clear. The witches had gone.

They both peered down into the tunnel. It was as black as night in there. It reminded Miranda of a ghost train she had once been in with her friend Susie. They had screamed their heads off from start to finish.

An old oil lamp stood just inside the entrance.

Pip picked it up. 'Hello, what's this?' He checked it over. 'This is just what we need.'

'What do you think it is, Pip?'

'I'll show you.' He lit a match and soon had it working.

The old oil lamp fizzled and spluttered, then shone brightly.

'That's better. There's no reason to be afraid now.'
'How did you guess?'
'Your face gave you away.'
'Oh, I see. Well, you don't have to worry about me now. I won't let you down.'
'I know that,' he said.
He held the lamp up high in front of him.
'C'mon, let's get this over with.'
'I'm ready when you are,' she said.

They took their first trembling footsteps into the tunnel of darkness. Huge cobwebs dangled down and tickled their faces as they passed. The light shone on strange creatures on the walls, and creepy crawlies could be heard scurrying about underfoot as the light brightened up their little homes. Two beady red eyes suddenly appeared out of the darkness. Miranda screamed, sending Pip into a panic. His hands shook so much he almost dropped the lamp.

The two beady red eyes had gone.

The light from the lamp grew dim then went out altogether. They were left standing there in the inky blackness. They both knew they could be attacked at any time. They were terrified of the unseen monster in their midst.

'Oh, Pip, please, don't leave me here to die.'
'Calm yourself, Miranda, brave hearts are needed here. We must keep going.'

She clung on to his coat tails as they stumbled blindly along. Daylight flooded in. The end was in sight.

'Look, Miranda. There's the way out of here.' C'mon.' They hurried eagerly forward.

The inky blackness faded and grew brighter until they could see where they were putting their feet. They were almost out when they saw a fearsome sight that held them breathless with terror.

A giant spider was in their midst and blocking their way out to freedom. It stood before them huge and terrifying in the shadows. Pip knew at once they were in a very dangerous situation. Miranda stared in fascinated horror, glued to the spot.

Pip was strangely silent.

'Do something,' Miranda hissed.

'I have never seen anything like it in all my life. What a beauty.'

They spoke in whispers.

'Are you mad?'

'Stay out of sight and I will see if I can get him to move.' His courage nearly failed him as he walked warily towards it. One glimpse from a beady eye and he knew it had seen him. 'I say, old chap,' said Pip, 'would you mind moving so we can get out of here?'

It scuttled forward.

'Eh, what's that?' bellowed the spider. 'You will have to speak up, I'm deaf.'

'Why, if it isn't my old friend Tommy,' cried Pip in amazement.

'Is that you, Pip, old friend?' cried the spider.

'What a surprise this is,' said Pip, with a wide grin.

They were overjoyed to see one another.

'Miranda,' called Pip, 'come and meet my friend Tommy Tickle.'

Miranda came warily out of the shadows to make his acquaintance. She couldn't help noticing they were both chatting happily away as if she didn't exist. They were quickly introduced.

Miranda found him charming.

'It is an honour to meet you,' said Tommy. 'Any friend of Pip's is a friend of mine. I must say I'm very surprised to see you here. It's not often I get visitors. Any chance you can you stay for tea?' he asked, hopefully.

'I'm sorry, we can't stay,' said Pip. 'We are in a dash of a hurry.'

'Why are you in such a rush to leave?'

Pip told Tommy what the witches had done. He explained everything in detail and left nothing out.

'And so you see,' added Pip. 'We must reach the castle before nightfall.'

'I had no idea things were as bad as this,' said Tommy. 'Let me give you both some advice,' he said, with an air of conspiracy about him. 'You must never look a witch straight in the eye or you will be turned to stone, and always try to look friendly, it may save your life.'

It was excellent advice they were given. They said their goodbyes and stepped out of the tunnel. They had arrived in the kingdom of witches.

The landscape was as bleak and unwelcoming as a wasps' nest. They stared at the witches' castle, which dominated the landscape. It stood high on a hill on the other side of a deep and dangerous river.

'What if someone sees us?' she whispered, staring up at the dark grey walls of the castle.

'They had better not,' he said.

They quickly made their way towards the water's edge and stared down into its murky depths. The river was like a raging torrent.

'We need a boat,' said Pip.

They could see at a glance there was nothing they could use.

'Pansy Poppet gave me some magic fairy dust that we could use,' said Pip, looking thoughtful. 'It might just work.' He searched in his little canvas bag that he wisely carried over one shoulder and brought out a tiny heart-shaped purse. 'Ah, here it is.' He threw the lot into the river and watched it disappear beneath the waves.

A boat suddenly appeared right in front of them. All they had to do was step into it. Pip grinned in delight.

Miranda's eyes grew big as saucers. 'I've seen everything now,' she cried in amazement.

'What a clever little fairy she is,' said Pip, with a wide grin. 'I must thank her when I get home.' He grabbed hold of the trailing tow rope that lay beside them on the river bank and held the boat steady. 'You get in first, Miranda,' and she quickly stepped into the small rowing boat.

Pip stepped lightly in after her and began rowing them across the river. It wasn't long before they were in trouble. The little boat rocked dangerously from side to side. The swirling current had them in its grip. They were in danger of drowning when a huge whale suddenly appeared.

'Quick,' he shouted, 'jump on my back and I will save you.'

They took a flying leap and landed on his back. They clung there like two little limpets as the whale swam with them to safety. They scrambled up the river bank as the boat sank beneath the waves. They both turned to thank the whale for saving their lives.

They saw the harpoon at once.

'Oh, look, Pip, he is hurt!'

'Who has done this dreadful thing?' cried Pip angrily.

'It was the witches,' cried the whale. 'I lost my way in a storm and am trying to find my way home.'

'You must let me help you.' Pip quickly pulled out the harpoon.

'Oh, I'm free. I'm free, at last I'm free,' he cried.
'We shall never forget you,' shouted Miranda, as the whale swam happily away.

CHAPTER NINE
THE LONELY GIANT

They were climbing steadily up the steep hill, when they casually glanced up. They saw the face of a giant looking down on them. A huge rock suddenly came hurtling towards them. They quickly jumped out of the way to avoid it and it missed them by inches.

'Just who does he think he is, throwing stones like that, he could have killed us,' cried Pip angrily. 'C'mon, Miranda, before he throws another one.'

'The nasty beast,' she muttered.

They quickly climbed to the top. The giant was waiting for them. He was a fearsome sight, and very angry.

'Visitors are not allowed,' he roared.

They both knew their lives were in terrible danger.

Miranda suddenly offered him a sweetie. 'Would you like a toffee?' she asked sweetly.

The giant peered cautiously into the sweetie bag that she held out for him. His eyes widened in surprise when he saw what was in there. 'Why, I don't mind if I do,' he said, taking one out. He popped a sweet into his mouth and began sucking on it noisily with great delight.

Miranda grinned at him. 'I knew you would like them. They are my favourite,' she said, taking one out for herself. 'Would you like one, Pip? The chocolate ones are the best,' she added.

Pip was too astonished to speak, but he took one anyway. Suddenly the giant burst into tears. He sobbed and sobbed as if his heart was breaking.

They were both alarmed.

'Whatever is the matter with you?' cried Pip. 'Are you in pain?'

The giant shook his head and began to speak in a very sad voice. 'In all my life, not one single person has ever shown me any kindness. And no one ever comes here, , not since the witches' castle appeared suddenly overnight, and everything changed. It used to be such a pretty place before the witches came, not bleak and barren like it is now. I hate them!' he cried. 'They have destroyed everything, even all the little animals that I used to play with have gone. I haven't a friend in the whole wide world. I am all alone.'

Pip suddenly realised the giant was harmless and meant them no harm. 'It must be awful to be all alone like that,' said Pip, with great sadness.

Miranda suddenly felt like crying.

'I would like to be your friend,' said Pip, suddenly looking up at him with a kindly expression on his face.

'Would you really be my friend?' cried the giant in delight.

'Oh, yes,' cried Pip. 'I would count it an honour to have you as a friend.'

'I would like to be your friend too,' said Miranda shyly.

'Oh, how wonderful,' cried the giant.

'I'm Pip and this is my friend Miranda.'

'My name is Peter,' said the giant, with a huge smile on his face. 'Would you mind telling me why you have come to this awful place?'

'Well, it's like this…' said Pip. He explained everything and left nothing out. 'So you see, Peter, we simply must get inside the witches' castle if we are to save The Magic Kingdom.'

'Do you really think you can do it?' Peter cried in astonishment.

'Will you help us, Peter?'

'I will,' he said. 'It so happens that I know of a secret entrance into the castle. Come on, and I will take you there.'

They sneaked up to the castle wall and quietly skirted around it. Peter put a finger to his lips and pointed to a huge boulder, which he quickly rolled aside as easily as if it were a little marble to reveal a small opening in the castle wall, just big enough for them both to squeeze through.

'I was searching for my pet rabbit, Rory, when I found it quite by chance,' whispered Peter sadly.

'Did you find him?' asked Miranda.

'No, I never saw him again. I think the witches caught him and roasted him for their supper.'

'I'm sorry to hear that,' said Pip.

'Yes, me too,' said Miranda.

They spoke softly in case the witches heard them. They had ears sharp as needles.

'When this is all over, we will come and seek you out,' promised Pip. 'And another thing,' he said, 'we won't forget how you have helped us; and you never know, perhaps we can return the favour.'

'I hope so,' said Miranda.

The giant looked down on them from his great height and felt a stirring of compassion that he had never expected to feel again. He was deeply moved by their bravery and wondered if he would ever see them again.

He quickly hurried off before they could see the tears in his eyes.

'Are you ready, Miranda?'

'I'm ready, Pip.'

'Let's get this over with then we can both go home.'

'I can't wait,' she said.

They climbed through the hole in the castle wall.

CHAPTER TEN
THE WITCHES' CASTLE

They were surrounded by witches. They were so close. Pip and Miranda could see the warts on their spiteful little faces. Nearby a big black cauldron bubbled merrily away. It gave off an awful pong. The witches suddenly saw them standing there.

They all turned to stare.

'Come to join the party, have you?' cackled a smelly witch.

'Plenty of meat on these bones,' cackled a greedy witch, with malicious glee.

'Two tasty morsels have arrived,' cackled another witch, wildly.

They cackled loudly – cackle, cackle, cackle; the evil sound echoed all around the castle walls.

They were having such fun.

'I seek audience with your queen,' cried Pip bravely. But he shook and trembled as he spoke.

'Do I hear a strange voice in our midst, sisters?'

A terrified murmur went up. She was their queen and the most feared witch of all time. One angry look from her and they would turn into marble statues. They quickly scurried out of the way.

Pip and Miranda watched her approach. She was the most frightening sight they had ever seen. They both knew they were in the presence of great evil.

'I suppose you are another one come to plead for someone's life,' she said, sounding bored.

'Nothing of the sort,' said Pip, bravely. 'I have a bargain to make.' He trembled in his little red boots.

'What could a little pip squeak like you have that I could possibly want?'

Pip reached into his bag and brought out the precious bottle of liquid.

He held it up for all to see. 'I have something you have desperately been searching for.'

'Oh, and what might that be?' asked the queen witch, cunningly.

'This little bottle contains the secret to eternal youth. Any witch who drinks from this bottle will be changed into the most beautiful witch that ever lived. Her beauty will outshine even the stars at night.'

The queen witch made a quick grab for the coloured bottle and tried to snatch it out of Pip's hand.

Pip quickly took a step back and kept a tight grip on it. 'Try that again and I will smash it into a thousand pieces.'

A ripple of murderous intent went around the crowd.

'What do I have to do?' she asked slyly.

'I want you to promise me as queen witch that you will leave The Magic Kingdom, forever, and take your witches with you when you leave. In return for our freedom, I will give you the secret to eternal youth.' He held it tantalisingly up just out of her reach. He could see she was seething with anger.

'Oh, is that all?' she said, her hate-filled eyes as black as night. 'I give you my promise as a witch that I will leave The Magic Kingdom, forever, and my sisters will depart with me.' She gave him a cunning look. 'I have kept my part of the bargain. Now hand it over.' She stretched out a withered arm with dirty black fingernails on a hand that looked as old as time itself.

Pip hesitated. I have a bad feeling about this, he thought, as he handed it over.

The queen witch snatched it out of his hand, pulled out the stopper, and began to greedily drink, glug, glug, glug. Pip and Miranda watched fascinated as she took her fill. There was great excitement in the air as everyone waited for the change to take place.

The queen witch turned a bright shade of green. She began to cluck like a hen. Then she whizzed around like a spinning top. Then suddenly it was all over.

She glanced at her reflection in the castle mirror. 'I am the same,' she spat at him viciously.

'You lied to me,' cried Pip in astonishment. 'You had no intention of keeping your promise. You will stay the ugliest witch of all time, and it's your own fault,' he cried furiously.

The mood began to change. The witches became very angry. The queen witch turned into a snarling fury, mad with rage, and smacked Pip a vicious blow to the head.

He fell to the ground stunned.

Miranda suddenly lost her temper when she saw what had happened. 'How dare you hit poor defenceless little Pip like that,' she yelled. 'I have a good mind to knock your block off and see how you like it. You are the worst bully I have ever seen and you are not going to get away with it!'

She turned on all the other witches with such sweeping vengeance.

'You should be ashamed of yourselves,' she cried furiously. 'You are all nasty bullies. BULLIES! BULLIES! BULLIES!' she cried, angrier than she had ever been in her whole life.

The witches suddenly trembled with fear. No one had ever dared to question their authority before. They were astounded at her bravery. She was completely fearless in their midst.

'BULLIES! BULLIES! BULLIES!' she yelled at them, without a thought for her own safety.

A strange magic began to take place.

The queen witch suddenly burst like a big balloon with a loud popping noise, and disappeared in a puff of grey mist. Loud popping noises could be heard as all the witches began to burst like balloons. POP! POP! POP! It went on, and on, and on, until every single witch had disappeared into thin air.

Pip and Miranda stared around them in baffled amusement and suddenly had fits of giggles and couldn't stop.

'I have never seen anything so funny in all my life,' Pip chortled.

They fell about laughing.

CHAPTER ELEVEN
THE RESCUE

'We must be quick if we are to save my friends,' said Pip. 'The castle will fall into ruin now the witches have gone.'

'Do you know where to look, Pip?'

'There's only one place they can be and that's in the dungeons that lie beneath the castle. Come on, Miranda, follow me.'

They hurried off.

They quickly found the entrance to the dungeons. It was very dimly lit with old lanterns in the walls that shed a grey ghostly light all around, but it was enough for them to see by. It was a long way down steep, stone steps until they reached the bottom.

It was a horrible place.

The air was damp and musty and smelled of rotten eggs. Rats scurried about the floor. A bunch of keys dangled from a nail in the wall. Pip quickly took them down and began to unlock their prison cell. Little faces peeped out between the prison bars. Pip could see how crowded it was; they were all tightly packed in like sardines in a tin.

'Is that you, Pip?' cried a voice.

'I have come to set you free,' he cried.

'It's Pip! It's Pip! It's Pip! He has come to save us!'

The voices rang out. The door was soon opened.

'Run for your lives!' shouted Pip. 'You must get out of here!'

They all rushed out.

Miranda watched them go with a sigh of relief. They all ran up the steps to freedom. Pip and Miranda were the last ones out. They ran from the castle and out into the fresh air. It wasn't long before great cracks began to appear in the castle walls. They watched as the castle walls begin to disintegrate until all that was left was a pile of dust and ruins.

The castle was gone.

'Good riddance,' said Pip smugly.

Miranda stood by, smiling. 'Job done,' she said.

They were suddenly confronted by an angry mob.

'Oh, Pip, where have you been all this time?' cried an angry little goblin.

'You don't give a butcher's knife about us,' cried a very cross little gnome.

'He thinks more of his fishing than he does about us,' cried a furious little elf, and they all joined in.

They all yelled at him.

Pip gazed at them in disbelief. This was not the kind of welcome he had expected.

'After all I've done, why you ungrateful wretches!' he cried. 'You have no idea what we have been through to save your miserable little necks.'

He told them all about their long and dangerous journey to save The Magic Kingdom, leaving nothing out.

'And what is more,' he added. 'If it hadn't been for dear Miranda here you would still be locked up in the prison dungeons at the mercy of those wicked witches. It is only her courage that has saved you all from a horrible death. And,' he added grimly, 'we could have been turned into stone statues at any time!'

There was a stunned silence.

They knew he spoke the truth and were very sorry for their behaviour in ever doubting him. They were suddenly very ashamed of themselves.

'Oh, Pip, can you ever forgive us?' they cried.

'I'm sorry, Pip. I'm sorry, Pip. I'm sorry too. We didn't mean it,' they all cried.

'Three cheers for Pip and Miranda,' shouted a pixie with a big smile on his face.

'HIP, HIP HOORAY, HIP, HIP HOORAY, HIP, HIP HOORAY!'

A loud cheer went up.

Thunder and lightning flashed across the sky. The sun began to shine.

'We can go home now,' said Pip. 'It's over.'

Happy smiling faces were everywhere. The fairy folk began to sing. It was the sweetest sound Miranda had ever heard. They all gazed into the distance as though expecting something to happen.

A beautiful rainbow suddenly appeared in the clear blue sky. It came slowly towards them like a brightly coloured ribbon to drop at their feet.

They all ran into the rainbow.

'What's happened to them?' cried Miranda in astonishment.

'They have gone home,' Pip said, smiling.

'I see,' she said thoughtfully.

'Come on, let's go and find Peter. We must tell him the good news.'

They hurried off to look for him.

The rainbow began to dissolve on the horizon until there was nothing left to see but empty blue sky and fluffy white clouds. They saw a lonely figure in the distance. They made their way over to him.

'Hi, Peter,' said Pip cheerfully. 'You'll be glad to know that all the witches have gone.'

'Why, that's wonderful,' he cried. 'Please tell me more.'

And Pip did just that. And he added, 'Do you know what Miranda did?'

Peter shook his head.

'She yelled at them and called them all bullies! You should have seen their faces, Peter!'

The giant guffawed and guffawed so loudly that the ground shook beneath their feet. Pip started to chuckle. He looked at Miranda, and she had a fit of giggles then burst out laughing too. The sound of their laughter rang out all over the hillside.

'Time for home,' said Pip, smiling.

'I wish I was coming with you,' said Peter, with such longing.

'We'd love to have you,' said Pip.

Peter stared at him in astonishment. 'Do you really mean it?' he cried. 'I can come with you and make my home in The Magic Kingdom?'

'You will be made very welcome.'

Peter gave a big toothy grin. 'In that case,' he said. 'I can't wait.'

Miranda had never seen anyone look so happy.

The three friends set off merrily down the hill. They hadn't gone far when they saw their friend the pilot with his little red helicopter waiting for them beside the river bank. They were very pleased to see him and greeted him warmly.

'This is Peter,' said Miranda cheerfully. 'He's going to make his home in The Magic Kingdom.'

'Oh, that is good news,' said the pilot warmly. 'I am very pleased to meet you, Peter.'

They all climbed into the little red helicopter. It was a bit of a tight squeeze but they all managed to fit nicely in and were soon on their way. They quickly flew over mountains, rivers and streams, on their way home. The snow was melting. They soon reached their destination. The pilot landed the helicopter in the soft green fields of The Magic Kingdom. They all climbed out and thanked the pilot for his help.

'Cheerio,' he called to them as he took off and disappeared into the cloudless blue sky.

'Goodbye, goodbye,' they chorused.

'There could never be a place as pretty as this,' cried Pip, looking around at all the beautiful scenery.

The sun was shining brightly. The blossom was on the trees. The grass was green with little daisies and buttercups popping up all over the place. The birds were singing merrily in the trees and all the woodland creatures wandered lazily about.

'Oh, Pip, what a wonderful place to live,' sighed Miranda, as she stared at all the flowers and magnificent scenery.

Peter was quite overcome by all the beauty around him.

They could hear a trumpet sounding their return and all the fairy folk came running from all directions to greet them. They could see Teddy Bear and Tommy Tickle; Rabbit Ears was bounding along beside him. Ivan, Pansy Poppet and Tiny grey mouse were there. Princess Aurora was waving gaily to them.

They were all delighted they were home.

Peter was warmly welcomed by everyone, and he knew he was going to be very happy in The Magic Kingdom.

CHAPTER TWELVE
PARTY TIME

'Let's have a party,' cried Pansy Poppet excitedly.

'Ooh! What a good idea. Why didn't I think of that?' said a sweet little pixie.

They were all very excited and everyone agreed it was a brilliant idea. They all hurried back to their new homes in the forest, which had all been re-built by magic.

The party was in full swing.

The trees were festooned with garlands and all around were little fairy lights. It was a magical time for all of them. The tables were laden with all sorts of delicious looking food. Miranda squealed in delight; it was a long time since she had seen jelly and ice cream. Peter's eyes were stretched wide in wonder at all the goodies spread out before him.

Pip was happy to be home.

Miranda was tucking into a big bowl of ice cream. Peter was laughing with a group of strong men as they played a game of tug-a-war. It was a hilarious situation just watching them. There was happiness all around. The party had been a roaring success.

It was a peaceful time.

Peter was resting nearby with a look of contentment on his face. The giant had never been so happy in all his life. Everyone had made such a fuss of him and he felt quite at home.

It was very late and everyone had gone home to bed.

Pip and Miranda were sitting beneath a huge oak tree chatting quietly together. They could see a star shining brightly in the sky.

'It's the wishing star,' cried Pip happily. 'We can make a wish and it will come true. I would like a new pair of boots,' he said, thoughtfully. 'My old ones are quite shabby. Is there something you would like, Miranda?'

'I would like to go home,' she said.

'You can come back any time you want,' said Pip. 'We would all love to see you again. You have a special place in our hearts and we shall never forget you.'

They both closed their eyes and made a wish.

Pip opened his eyes to find the magic had worked. On his feet were a new pair of shiny red boots, and he was delighted. He glanced at Miranda, who had fallen into a deep sleep beside him. He gave a secret smile. 'Goodbye, dear friend. Until we meet again,' he said wisely.

CHAPTER THIRTEEN
SAFE HOME AGAIN

Miranda woke up in her own little bed at home.

Her mother was calling to her. 'Get up, lazy bones or you will be late for school.'

She climbed out of bed and quickly dressed. She remembered her dream about a strange land and a little elf. She was putting her shoes on when she saw the flute lying on the window sill beneath her window.

She smiled softly to herself. It hadn't been a dream after all, and one day she would see Pip again. Their friendship would last forever.

She ran downstairs. 'Coming, Mummy,' she called cheerfully.

THE END

Lightning Source UK Ltd.
Milton Keynes UK
UKHW012003300522
403739UK00003B/526